Dancing Naked
in Front of Dogs

Dancing Naked in Front of Dogs

collected poems

2014 – 2018

Michael Maul

Dancing Naked in Front of Dogs
Copyright © 2018 by Michael Maul

Cover art: Sabourin Graphic Design

Layout and page design: Sharon Maul

ISBN: 9781731185464

First Edition

For news about other projects Michael Maul is currently involved in, to read new poems, schedule readings or speaking engagements, visit his website at *www.michaelmaul.net.*

CONTENTS

CHAPTER ONE

CHAPTER TWO

CHAPTER THREE

CHAPTER FOUR

CHAPTER ONE

Anniversary Poem

I stood on the sidewalk
by my parents
when my brother set off
on his first bike ride solo around the block
and never came back.

For fifty years some of me has waited there
midway through his lap,
but his journey continues as he learns firsthand
lessons in how the universe expands.

We had no way to know
where he would go:
no pins in a map to show
a suspicious freezer in someone's garage,
or a hit and run by a car,
or a hyperbaric collection sack
in the belly of a ship to Mars.

What I know now
(but then did not)
is many moments come and go,
but really bad ones stay.

They have made me live with the remains
of a child heart in the frame of an aging man,
trying still to negotiate with something
a slightly better version of forever,
scaled down so not to ask too much,
hoping less enough could be approved.

Like meeting in a halfway place,
he in a soft knit shirt I outgrew,
and I, promising not to talk,
just remain side by side with him
in our own space,
kickstands down, and sidewalk safe.

Chasing the Ex

Today I ran into an earlier wife.
Twenty years of life had passed
since we escaped a marriage
that could not survive even one.

She began, to me, as a person of interest,
who later became my first responder.
We recognized each other only barely,
standing on the outer rim
of a bookstore talk.
And, fittingly, exchanged few words
before re-parting.

Yet the clatter went on inside my head.
I was, back in our day, fascinated by the way
she wrote messages in lipstick
on mirrors or countertops
before she left for work,
perfumed words barely
once removed from her lips,
that sank in
when I tried to wipe them off.
Whether "wash my car"
or "take me away again."

There were times back then
when she smiled at me
and the world went quiet.

Then came the end,
when we moved to motions of
half-hearted love.
And once bright lips became laden clouds,
high and low, that parted one day to say
"I no longer feel amazing."
And to herself she sighed and said,
"I have brighter days ahead."

By which, unsympathetically,
I thought she decided somehow
to become more intelligent now.

Finally, I recalled being kissed awake.
About her I also remembered that,
and never after our lips parted
have I since woken in that place.

Now my life has less surprises:
except for my shoes,
sole mates that hide themselves at night
and I find again to start each day.

After I turned off the light,
I stewed in her juices
for the rest of the night
admitting, at dawn
and years too late,
the possibility of making a mistake.

That what I thought I was, but then became
were not really both the same,
old enough now to see
no lights from days up ahead
shining even half as bright
as those I saw in her,
and she saw, once, in me.

Wedding Bouquet

She caught it, though short and slow and wide,
to the disappointment of full-gene ingénues,
who shuffled perfectly off the dance floor.
Confused, flowerless confections. Wondering
how the world goes wrong like this
on a such special day.

The deejay tried to nudge the moment on
but she stood there still holding her place,
looking at the bouquet that had fallen into her hands
like manna from heaven, a peace offering perhaps
for a lifetime of Down syndrome,
ready for whatever was supposed to happen next.

And what came was the Maid of Honor, who led her off
and borrowed the flowers back
while the mother of the bride
organized a hasty "re-do,"
as if a goofy family pet had wandered in
to a wedding portrait, ruining a memory
perfectly posed.

As the other girls returned to the dance floor
this time she waited on the side,
smiling through the re-do,
fascinated by the lingering feel satin ribbon had left
across her hands,
and at hearing, for the first time,
the seductive voice of flowers
calling her on to bigger dreams
that good weddings and lifted hearts
seem to always bring.

Malaysia Airlines Flight MH17
Shot Down by a Russian Missile
Over Eastern Ukraine, 2014

Don't forget to show hospitality to strangers.
For some who have done this have entertained
angels without realizing it.

Hebrews 13: 1-2

Angels dressed as passengers wearing blankets,
having overcome the broken wings,
are the ones still ascending.
While below, all the insides of their earthbound lives
have exploded like fumbled melons,
open and giving back
seeds of ambition and troubled love
mixed with ash and dust of bone
still floating to earth without urgency,
in a measured sifting
along the long earth gashes,
mass graves slowly filling
under hushed and chilling stars.

Returning to Hunan University

In the autumn, just south of Dongting Lake,
when the air cools and rains abate,
I return to study at Yuelu Academy.

Along the way I steep myself in flavors of Hunan;
cucumbers first whacked with the flat of the cook's bat
and soaked in chili, garlic, vinegar and sesame oil,
mixing the lake's cool mist with indescribable heat
of the *guai wei jiang*.

Chairman Mao, Hunan's favorite son,
knew the inner power of our food,
counseling comrades that
the more chilies they eat,
the more revolutionary they would become.

As I walk I feel a heat rise inside
where roots of knowledge begin to grow,
awakening burning dreams of what I can be,
deep, deep inside this Hunan man I am.

Ruining The Cuddle

It is a widely-known curse
of over-thinking,
asking questions that ruin things.
So, cuddling after a bountiful bout
I inquire, "Why am I being held?"

"What?"
"I have a right to know."
"Okay... uh, maybe because you are impossibly
adorable?" she replied.
And I felt her arms tighten at my sides.

But we were not lovers, really.
Not sweethearts, partners or even close friends.
Meaning, as I saw it,
I was being held now without bond.

Which I point out.
But then she wants to know
"What? Are you calling me a slut?"
Causing her to break the cuddle
and gather up to go.

Her demeanor hardens then
as all words abruptly end.
And a conversation,
that moments ago seemed just fine,
with no warning, just flatlines.

Body Heat

You slide out of bed early
on this bitter November day
and under the darkness of covers I find
a cache of warmth you left behind.

Black outside and in, and half asleep
I trace your shape with my bare skin
feeling where you begin to become
an invisible girl woven into linen.

I lay over the space your body saved,
a crime scene silhouette
covered by a sheet,
then hear the water shut off and your shower end.

I roll back to my own spot again
and rejoin a more literal world,
that has little patience for poetry beds
like this,
where at once you exist and don't,
in the waning warmth and bloodless heat
of a disembodied lover.

No Cover Art

Devoid of cover art, I write with a colony of words,
who show up everyday like black worker ants
willing to live or die in a heap on the page
if I say the cause is just, if I give hope
of our building something good today.

Not everlasting, necessarily, but magnificent enough.
Like a life-sized veined cow carved from butter,
or household furniture hewn of ice,
or dragons drawn in chalk climbing from the walk,

or on the beach, a wheelchair man made of sand
with sun-colored grainy knees
with no past or future but to be swept away today,
in a fabricated hat
of woven water reeds.

Watching Me Falling in Love

You walked through my apartment
talking of art for the walls and custom drapes,
and the plight of wilting
dehydra plants on plates.

But that's the way here lately it's been.
Shallow and dry.
So as you spoke
of potting soil and watering sticks,
I saw my face in the round mirror
on the wall by where you stood.

I was appalled at how I held my head,
posed like a daytime drama hack:
eyes slightly squinted but yet bright,
my jaw set strong and lips parted,
wetted right.

It was the face of me,
undeniably,
involved in some early stage
of falling in love.

I knew this is what men do
to impress a woman
who matters like you.

I was gently directed back
to your horticultural talk
but could do little more
than nod at the floor,
as if actually weighing
the words you are saying.

While inside I'm looking
at the child I am,
feeling an urge toward you
to extend my hand
as if we are walking partners on a fieldtrip,
who seriously took the teacher's admonition
to keep each other safe
during excursions away from school.
And just like that
inside I feel the pendulum
begin to swing,
away from living spaces
back to living things.

A Face to Die For

I.
Basically I'm on my way to kill my mother, Ruth.
Undetected passing over one end of America to the other
above the clouds, an angel of death
looking for the specific street and house.

I was bidden by my brother, who phoned in updates
of her slow auguring into earth,
finding her path to dying, but not yet the one to death.

"I think she's waiting for you," he said.
"You need to come out here so she lets go."

II.
My mother was always reluctant
to go anywhere without me
chatting on the way to visit friends
when I was still too young to be in school.

She was speechless now, though her body soldiered on.
In her bed she extended an arm, as if I were a beau,
or here to help her find a seat
only moments before the show.

"She wants to hold your *hand!*"
My brother sounded piqued.
"Oh, OK. I didn't understand."

III.
We spent her last hours in pantomime:
locked gazes, smiles, deep in the language of the hands.
We all waited around her bed
as if it were docked at a pier,
waiting for a mother ship
to spirit her away.

IV.

"Angels come" she whispered weakly near the end.
And I raised my hand.
For here I was, both first born
and last beckoned for.
A dark angel now,
in one hand a heart,
in the other a scythe to cut her down,
feeling pain she must have felt
when she brought me in
and that I felt now at being tapped
to guide her out.

V.

It took an hour to depart.
She, to a new place behind the sun.
And I, back to my earthly life
that she'd begun and left to me
still undone.

I wobbled down a narrow hall
and wandered out,
feeling numb and wondering
what this last half-life
would be about.

Willing to trade the world
for one final chat
just to hear her whisper back
and tell
what for.

Back to School

Just like that,
my son killed the crosswalk kiss.
I knew it loomed, but not so soon.
He just ran away and waved his hand,
passed in front of crossing guards
and then went in.

Among parents still hugging their kids
I pretend to wave goodbye
to a boy
not only out of sight,
but already gone.

In the Photo

In the black and white photo I now hold
of you before we met,
I see over your shoulder and out of focus
lights on an ornamented Christmas branch,
helping me find an anchor in time.

You were sitting in a chair I do not recognize,
nor do I know whose house you're in,
but the smile I see is genuine.

Then I think how long it's been
since seeing you.
And recall the feel of your hair in my hands,
of touching the edge of your sweater cuff.
And remembering even deeper in
how flustered you became one night
answering a question I lightly asked,
cupping your hands around my ear and reddening
as you whispered in
your seldom shared middle name.

Getting Something Off Her Chest

She wanted to get something off of her chest,
then confided she hated her breast.
What did I think?

I was, at first, too saddened to speak.
"It's the one that you have left.
How is it not best?"

Of course there are reasons. I understand
feeling betrayed already by one now gone,
turning your ire on its twin
though for nothing it has done.

Or perhaps you are distancing yourself from it now,
in case cancer returns
to get in again under your skin.

What I hope most is not the case
is you being dissatisfied
after comparing yourself to the human race.

Tall or short, fat or thin,
we are the only thing we have.
Your breast (a survivor, too,) or buns, or neck or hands
are all one you, who we admire and deeply love.

You deserve good things.
Hating yourself in pieces and bits
has no place upon that list.

Evidence of Falling Leaves

Across the breakfast table
looking down at the newspaper spread
you ask me when
autumn begins this year.

Out the window
I see a colored leaf from
the spindly tree in our backyard
drift down like a blood-red boat
pitching to the river floor.

I cannot look away,
recalling the Lakota people
telling a similar story one day,
whose dancers used
cupped and painted hands
to be falling leaves before my eyes

"I don't know," I answer.
Unsure of what just began.

CHAPTER TWO

Dancing Naked in Front of Dogs

They've never seen anything like this before.
They are enwrapped at me unwrapped,
wanting to know more.
At first, if they were in danger.
And next, if I was in distress,
descended on, perhaps, by bees?

The Elder reassures The Younger.
Satisfied all is right, they sit as still
as a brace of bronze greyhounds
guarding a Victorian door.

Meanwhile I sway and twirl away.
"This is beautiful," Younger dog wants to say.
"There you have his wild side," Elder replies.
"All these years," he said, shaking his head,
"who knew what was trapped inside?"

Fred Astaire Studio

"I am no dancer," I said.
But the teacher started the music.
Already chastened twice
I begin to stalk you like a wrestler.

The part of my heart that brought me here
starts to reconsider and, embarrassed, averts its eyes
with timing so poor that for a moment I freeze upright,
arms extended, like a statue of someone
welcoming home a long-lost child.

Yet I keep coming, believing I may corner
still my stubborn dream,
that rhythm can make us click,
like two coach horses prancing in a hitch,
showing in metaphor, I can stay with you,
step-for-step.

Partner not predator.
Dying here on my feet just to hold you
in front of everyone inside
this bright-lit classroom ring tonight.
And perhaps in future days,
on a vastly wider public stage,
in more graceful and lasting ways.

Sunday Clothes

For fifteen years I've walked the same path to church.
Along an early morning county road
strewn with fallen car parts,
broken bottles and, here and there,
hastily tossed underwear.

Who lives these feral lives while I'm snug in bed?
Or have roadworthy bras and briefs
escaped from my own dark dreams,
throwing themselves headlong into traffic instead?

Or (I literally stop to consider)
may a naked woman be up ahead
who, after draining a final beer and stubbing out a smoke,
slips off her clothes and slowly strolls,
inviting me to overtake,
instead of sliding in a pew?

Quickening my pace, I feel my heart begin to race.

Hand Knitting

The sadder my mother became
(what she called blue phases)
the more sweaters we received.
As she worked through her depression
to a knit one, purl one, rock-rock beat,
they began to pile up.

Though she is now decades gone
and they were knit
to fit a teen
I've kept one,
to remind myself
how accomplished she became.

Which has nothing to do
with sweaters and yarn.

But to help me recall how lives can be changed
by simple things.
Two small hands.
Common threads.
Sticks and string.

Remnants

Young or old, by the time they get to me
these dogs have already taken
the long way.
Their path to my door passes first
through adult daughters and sons,
whose new circumstances
(college, babies, careers, divorce)
conspire to make impossible dogs.

In the air, they can smell the change.
They trot to the cupboard where I keep boxed treats,
while sneaking sideways peeks
into corners where they could sleep,
or glance down hallways toward shuttered rooms.

Then I lay a blanket on the floor and
the new dog begins to scratch and bunch,
dig and pile and adjust, lifting corners
with its mouth or plowing furrows with its snout.

And lays down when complete, exhaling in relief,
signaling the change is done:
he has a space and still someone.

So on we live, in good-natured ways
through happy-enough dog and people days,
some touched by sickness, some by age.
But at the door
we stretch
and each day begins
when, leash in hand, and one by one
we all step out again.

A Body of Work

Even when it's time to go,
the body of one's work
stays behind.
Cut and stitched and scarred,
burned and healed
and then burned again.
What the mind forgets,
skin remembers and reminds.

He wore it out at sixty-nine.
Years of working in factories and on farms
breaking fingers along the way,
his heart and both his arms.

And if other eyes are like mine,
in what is left behind they can see on him
a fossil record of his days on earth,
calling forth some simple odes.

To poverty.
Disability.
Struggling to work.
But not to balancing labor with fun
back when choices were basically none.

Sackafice

"I'm not askin you to sackafice nothin,"
dad used to say to mom.
But, of course, there is always sackafice
when there's too little meat on the bone.

Yet there were also stories of their great passion,
how after a tiff, he would shine her shoes at night
while she slept, him always claiming
a miracle in the morning light.

Which made her, who knew better,
and we small kids (who did not)
all feel chosen
and never alone.

Music To My Ears

Hovered over ivory, my fingers
feel for music flowing below,
like a blackbird tracking
a worm with its feet,
or a dowser tracing
underground streams.

Tonight I find and follow a new seam,
coaxing and cajoling music up,
from inside feelings to outside sound
that, once freed,
lays down like a necklace on a velvet gown.

The music had to first consent
to be unearthed before delivering itself
into hands, trusting me to tell its tale,
correctly, with honesty that rings
and, just in case, with grace notes
ready in the wings.

To The Little Girl Who Kissed My Dog

You did not, it is clear, learn
such behavior from your mother.
Who shouted in the park
as if she knew too well
all bad things that can accrue
to girls who follow their hearts.

Fingers bitten,
faces scratched,
germ attacks.
You did not care.
Nor, apparently,
easily scare.

Yours will be a better life than hers.
And you are right to not eat everything
she puts in front of you.
Fear, after all, is a life-long meal,
that once begun your choices are two:
you feed on it,
or it feeds on you.

The Son in My Face

I am remembering when
you used to sleep on my stomach
like we were in a cartoon:
your baby body rising and falling
with each breath I took,
balanced above my belly like
a floating feather.

I would lie on my back,
and look up like a strong man in a circus act,
holding you out, and smiling
into the bright son shining.

I have a picture of it.
Before you grew.
Before I divorced your mother,
changing everything you knew

and began standing on the front porch,
ringing the doorbell
of our home.

Breakfast Alone Near the Shore

At seventy-five I am near the age
when it is possible
to stop thinking about myself.
Instead, to see things for what they are:
a cloth napkin folded into an obelisk on the table,
a fellow diner's warming smile.

The midmorning sun has made
a charcoal sketch in silhouette
on the wall near where I sit.

Outside, a waterspout of shorebirds
corkscrew their way into the blue sky
in a helix string.

Hot tea steaming next to my hand.
A thick beige cup.
A thimble of honey
placed by its side.
Perfection without excess.

And I am blessed at seventy-five.

The Clothes of Children Claimed by Fire

*A remembrance of the 1988 Carrollton, Kentucky
crash, for years the highest casualty bus-accident in
America.*

It was a hot start to summer in early May
when Kentucky church kids on a bus
were trapped inside a fiery crash,
igniting what was already a warm night outdoors
into a 2,000 degree day inside,
turning children, upholstery, rubber and steel
into fifty-nine candles on a blazing cake.

Not many days thereafter
the victims' parents began to show
at Christian missions and Kingdom Halls
arms full with empty clothes,
as if babies had slithered out,
through arm sleeves or legs of jeans
like tunnels in a McDonald's PlayPlace
before being caught mid-air
by the quick hands of God.

But here, where there is not enough
of anything,
we know what the right thing is
but are too poor to do.

So unlike the children who are lost,
these clothes of kids claimed by fire
would be resuscitated,
and readied to go on living.

For days we laundered stains
until the last of stubborn grass
and earth and trees trapped
on elbows, chests and knees
gave up what hid within common thread.

Then the clothes were folded and boxed
and, on a Sunday, given to the living poor.
Where parking lots filled early
as next-to-nothings formed a somber line
in the hope to see or touch or own
garments transmogrified, closer to God,
with value beyond measure
in this otherwise
worn-out, threadbare world.

Frank Intense

I forget what it was called.
Jade East or English Saddle something.
Whatever it was, when it came to fuming
Frank's incense knew no bounds.

At his house, in his car,
eating al fresco
whether or not he was even there,
he seemed always in the air.

He would say they are fragrances
girls were crazy for back when,
and though now old,
helps them feel that young again.

"What if they don't like it anymore?" I asked.
He just shrugged then.

"It doesn't matter either way.
How I smell is who I am."

Robert Penn Warren: Elegy & Reminiscence

Near Hocking River shores,
near the foothills of the Appalachian chain,
near old homes that looked
the same as where he was born,
I shared a southern breakfast
with Robert Penn Warren.

He sat down to visit and dine
with a few promising students
and me at the time.

At twenty I was the youngest to accept
an invitation to eggs and biscuits,
ham gravy and grits
with this Southern man of letters,
winner of two Pulitzer Prizes,
who traveled with a walking stick.

On that morning,
after quiet table chats, left and right,
one-by-one we'd say our names,
and share opinions
on theories of criticism of the day.

After the meal when settings were cleared
we made our ways across the floor
awkwardly toward where Robert Penn Warren
waited to shake hands at the door.

[...]

Mine was the last he clasped,
which he held tight
while repeating my names, given and sur.
Then, leaning in, out of nowhere proclaimed:
"I try to write every morning.
I think about nothing at all,
to see just what falls in."

"Thank you," I replied.
He smiled, turned and ambled out,
our encounter at an end.

I walked toward class while looking back
at welcome words left on my plate:
that writing was still possible for those of us
with nothing waiting in their heads.

I never saw him another time
but eleven years later read
he won his third Pulitzer Prize,
in nineteen hundred and seventy-nine.

Robert Penn Warren lived ten years more
before he finally passed.
I was writing through my middle ages by then
and he was eighty-four.

If I could speak to him again
I'd begin by noting he changed my life
on the single day that he was in.

I don't know what else that day he did
after passing on to me
advice I innately grasped,
but his words invited wondrous things
that daily still drop by.

In his absence, year on year,
we have built a community here
of poems and stories,
ideas, words and phrases,
characters and names
that I now have learned to live among
and know the rules of their domain.

So thank you to Robert Penn Warren.
Because of what he wrote and uttered,
today I live a writer's life,
of persistent wonder.

The Frère Jacques Men's Chorus

I went to the try out only because of the name
and the promise that no one wishing to participate
would be turned away.

The first practice lasted two days,
which we used to memorize French words
that not even the director knew.

Removed from meaning to English ears,
they became just sounds and rhymes
that, when I closed my eyes, swept me away

to a congregation in another land
arriving early to hear us sing
jammed into pews
and cheering us through
even verses we tried to wing.

CHAPTER THREE

Germantown
For Walter Reis

Women, shaped like pigeons,
dressed in black cotton calico,
clop the sidewalk on feet swollen-in
to Old World square-heeled shoes.

Pragmatic, boar bristle
bearded men austere,
sit straight to eat
then scrape the crumbs beside their plates
into geometric shapes.

They live where there is no greater sin
than to suffer foolishness.
At night they write by candlelight
the names of those who come and go,
on a ledger they keep Bible sewn
between the Testaments Old and New,
bound in leather and near at hand.

But there,
among these farriers,
carpenters and breakers of land,
was my German grandfather
who instead of any useful thing
taught his kids to dance and sing.

He was a virtuoso who labored in an orchestra pit
playing gastric tuba sounds for vaudeville skits
and, for silent film,
wrote notes beautiful enough
to earn the leading lady's kiss.

Of all of them in Germantown
I am from this:
one who found melody in sound.

[...]

And coming home with lamplights lit,
in his pockets broken chocolate bits,
he sat on our beds and held our hands
then sang us back to sleep, one-by-one,
with lullabies he wrote for each.
This man, less valuable than bumper crops
or fine shaped wood, but more rare:
a man beautiful like music.

Occasional Writing

There is a special handwriting
of an occasional nature
that I reserve
for singular times.

For adding "Love,"
the year and my first name
below a purchased saccharine line.

I use power strokes
to show strong emotion
which, on normal days, I forego.

Then I hand
what I have signed
with a gift
to one who knows me
and the life we've lived well.

She, whose special skill
is to sort right through
shapes and spaces
and love implied,
to keep the truth
and discard disguise.

Blueberry Sorting

I watch as you stand at the sink,
engaged in blueberry sorting.
They are in good hands,
instantly separating ones right for you
from those that will not go forward:
each blueberry in a balancing act,
then dispatched, to heaven or hell.
You do it well.

I look on and wonder if it's a skill
you first perfected while sorting out
your ended marriage
that you now apply to other things.

Or is it just the opposite?
Is blueberry experience where you learn first
to separate what you only favor
from what you know is love?

For some it's easier to see from far away,
like the view from space between people,
which finds and focuses on what's not there.
But your way of knowing is closer in;

weighing and turning what's in your hands,
flesh on flesh, cautious not to confuse again
decomposition with tenderness,
or mistake a moment when
the sweet to rotten-ripe begins.

It is the hardest way.
I see in the bend of how you stand,
your thin bruise-colored skin
wrist-deep in a pan of blueberries;
bathing then blotting what you picked.

As you dry your hands then wipe the knife
I hear a deep breath drawing in,
then your voice say, would I like to stay?
I answer, yes, then begin to wonder
what conversation we are in.
Staying for berries?
Staying the night?
or staying, perhaps, for the rest of my life?

Reuniting with Old Friends While Sunbathing in Florida

Sunning together brings out the rest in people:
a mixture of bad breaks and mars,
like blows landed out of the blue,
from malevolent forces
behind the stars.

Seldom aired openly over the years,
just when we think we've seen it all,
annual trips to the shore reveal
new twists and turns,
laid bare on those we thought we knew.

Apparently more difficult said than shown,
scars don't wait for stories to be told,
but get to the point surgically:
old friends have new designs on their skin,
like sketched up battle plans
in fights to stand or walk or run.

Like scrimshaw carved
into tusk or bone,
these are folk art scenes of life:
from knees replaced to chests
cracked wide then woven back,
arriving home wearing fresh blue line tracks,
then picking up pieces
of interrupted lives.

So year out, year in,
I travel to the beach again
to see new sites of things unseen.
Whether hosted in old friend ankles,
backs, throats or hands,
it's always something new
when once simple lives
before your eyes
start to be unsmooth.

To My Students
*(Frustrated with Learning English
 as a Second Language)*

I should not be teaching this course,
a subject without beginnings, middles or ends;
a mother tongue which at the end of most days
I don't understand.
Though so far I've given answers back
to all the tricky questions asked:

Y is both a letter (no, not the kind that you can mail)
and a question.

Yes, all the days in the week do have names but,
no, the one after Saturday is not pronounced
"Someday."

No, a smart man and a wise guy are not the same
things.

No, angina pain is not a condition restricted to women.

No, U-haul is not a state.

Why do some people call liking something "taking a
cotton to it?" This is unanswerable.

There is no such thing as a Grey Wall of China.
Doesn't exist. Ask your Asian classmates.

Yet feeling bewildered and wanting something solid to hold onto, I understand. Those students I refer to the class description section of the Course Catalogue:

You're in a big country in which native-speaking people make a living on TV explaining what other native-speaking people are saying. Here, almost no one understands anybody. So in the end you will find your way into English alone. You will learn to listen, speak and imitate. These three things, above all else, will help you find a job, disguise your soul, and then assimilate.

Moving Parts
For Uncle Fen

First it was your heart that went,
moved to a forty-six year old father of five.
Your kidneys then
(to someone's twenty-three-year-old son.)
Then came your donated lungs
and a list of bones, tendons,
nerve sheaths, veins
and unburned skin to different lives.

Like a pea shuffled beneath walnut shells
then disappearing, your organs became
a game of moving parts.
But it's what you wanted.
Not to be buried, but be the melting snowman
who disappears when its season ends.

And today you are all in,
cornea to ligaments,
turning one life into many
like feeding five-thousand with two fish.

Always a man of many layers,
you blended in
to a crowd of women and men
who have made you more than your sum.
Ending the game perfectly,
with nothing to discard from your hand.

The last to leave were easy parts:
the car to a niece,
your clothes to Goodwill.
The device from Medical Arts, that you wore
around your neck, went to me.

A *LifeSaver 2000* suspended at the end
of a nineteen sixties rainbow lanyard.
Just a simple button hanging down,
red and round,
promising the wearer instant access
to hope inside this world
or, on the outside,
lasting peace.

Old Shirt Paint

There is nothing we imbue with memory more
intimately than the worn stories of our clothes ...
wearable micro-museums woven of both love and loss.
                                        Maria Popova

Divining from runes and sorcery is not for me.
One ruined shirt shows all I need to know
about who I was, and what I will be.

For years it has come out on special occasions,
painting projects mostly, where new drips build
and blend into now epic spills.

Some of the colors, like old tunes or oven scents,
pull me back into rooms and times I spent
with people who helped me paint, then shared my bed.

I've come to believe in paint,
and in the difference colors make
from all the years I've slung and rolled
while dreaming simple dreams
of better couches, cars or clothes.

What has come and gone since then
still lives in little places
on this shirt,
a lifetime of starts and stops, shapes and shades
that have somehow interlaced to make lasting sense.

As the brushes and drop cloths come out again,
and paint lids pop, I hear old shirt paint begin
to whisper my heart awake, as if coaxing a stubborn
child:

Shhh, come lift your wrinkled head.
It's time for colors new. No need to wait.
Oh, what a difference these will make!

Open Borders

Snowflakes arrive
on American shores
(The Weather Channel shows)
from systems that began
in China, in Vietnam,
and the urban prefectures of Japan.

Piling up in Kanji script
each character is
a different story
coming down

stacking one atop the next
falling in a flurry
of urgent pleas
that become cold tears
when they reach my skin.

They are early casualties
of a season known
for bitter breezes
that this year first feed
on the silent hopes of women and men
from eight thousand miles drifting in.
We watch them arrive
fall and end
inches from our outstretched hands.

What Trees See

In the spirit of full transparency
I'll acknowledge
I do not know what trees see.
For unlike potatoes
(though similarly grounded)
trees live entire lives
without the benefit of eyes.

But trees I've known and re-seen
after my absence of many years
at least would be
old enough to recognize me.

Then, again, who knows.
Even if trees saw,
how much could they really recall?

I enquire because there are things
I've done in the presence of trees
that if they noticed and still knew,
would have disappointed them in me.

Things that happened with others
in woods or at the cemetery's edge
when I was a young man, on summer nights,
when roots were shallow and not set.

Yet trees, of all things,
should understand,
and be the first to forgive
youth's shortfalls.

On the way to their own full height
trees leave behind a history all their own
of comporting themselves in reckless ways:
as saplings wrapping fence posts in their limbs
or piercing the cab and growing up
through the roof of an abandoned truck.

These mistakes, of trees, are plainly seen.
Mine, at least, are breaking down
between the pages of an unread book,
not gone, but fading.
Regretted still, but finally waning.

Hypothetical Fetus

Before Google calendar sharing,
you made a little book to carry
in your purse to plot your periods
and check days most safe to grant
timely pleas for sex.

The goal back then
was chasing pleasure purely,
while sparing ourselves
being drawn into third-person living.
Which from one thoughtless night
can grow from wham and bam to sonogram
and a family of coincidence.

You were afraid that if we'd slip,
and contractions ever began
you would be the one pushed out
of college, a career and all the dreams
you held so dear.
But your calendar, a trusted map,
led us all around that trap.

Though now
I think we may have betrayed ourselves
with cleverness,
losing in the grass
happiness others seemed to grasp,
on a path to parenthood they either chose
or drunken-stumbled in.

Today they surround our lives,
all more richly fertilized,
and I wonder at what
we failed to conceive?

Had we not been so unfettered then,
would we still have drifted off
in different ways?

Or noticed, as sloops and skiffs
ladened with love ungiven
slipped away in foggy haze,
casting off other things in their wake:
icebergs bobbing and bitter days.

What Haunts Us Most

It was bad timing.
Exactly the kind of thing grief will do:
watching my aunt lowered down
and feeling relieved
now we won't have to tow
an empty coffin home.

We'd put down her bluetick hound
only two weeks before.
Said good-bye,
then drove back from the vet
with an empty crate,
door ajar, banging inside the car
like a storm-blown gate.

And so life goes those crazy days:
a tiny aunt disappears underground
and along the way
her haunting dog has learned to stay.

Rio Dulce

On the way to the calm waters
in a Guatemalan hurricane hole,
we sail on a sweet river, Rio Dulce,
past Children's Island
home to one hundred and five
orphaned lives.

Rio Dulce's safety flows
beyond the reach of child eyes
viewed from the dry strip of land
where only children grow.

After thirty years
of war in a row,
soft Caribbean winds
have pushed hard
on their fragile skin,
separating bloom from stem.

As we slip past
they dot the shoreline
in faded color clothes,
like a patch of wild orchids,
lovely at a distance
but, we know, unlikely to grow
vivid or rich
as the cared for, hand-raised kind.

Spring Cuttings

The dogwoods remind it is a season of blood.
Inevitably the first spring cuttings
of roadside grass and bladed yards
level also tiny snakes and rabbit nests
as the Gravely mower munches on,
still hibernation starved.

In its wake are feather, fur and hollow bone
awash in new blood,
and grasses clipped and tipped in red,
hor d'oeuvres of pagan spring.

A time of promise,
a time to sacrifice prey,
before claws and teeth are set,
before vulnerable skin is camouflaged,
before birds have learned why to fly,
and rabbits why to run.

CHAPTER FOUR

A Reporter's Poem on the Occasion
of an Autistic Girl's Death in Toronto

For two days a thousand people searched,
authorities, families, the hordes who hoped
to find a girl only half frozen by the winter,
with maybe toes and fingers lost
but essential things enough remaining
to be barely coaxed to life.
But you, you would not be found,
and we began returning finally,
each with no autistic girl to warm.

I went and waited in the morgue
for the family to identify your form.

> "Is this the right frozen girl?
> Have we been talking about the same one
> all this time?"

> "Yes."

Watching you on that table of hard endings
I hoped you might seize this moment
to thaw out utterly,
rise up from this ordeal
no longer numb, but full of words,
gushing ideas and scoldings overdue.

But the facts are, you chose a different end
and threaded through women and men.

To reach darkness at the tunnel's end,
you evaded an army of women and men.

My Kind
Meditations On Cross Talk

Sometimes I wonder where it is
when it goes from me, my kind.
Leaving me for days
with brittle thoughts
in moments when I need it most.

Later, when my kind comes back like a hungry cat,
it begins to mend coarseness that it finds.
The world needs no more cruel or hardened faces.
But if they must be, I pray it's not me
who resides inside those cold, dark places.

Things I Know for Semi-Sure

There is no better metaphor
for our relationship than our asses:
mirror images of each other
separated by dark crevasses.

It's true.
And, yes, you may want to fight,
but deep inside
you know I'm right.

Dried Dates

It was the married daughter who posted my picture
in an online dating site for older Christian singles.
Reminding me that the death of a partner
is not just the end of things loved now lost,
but the beginning of all familiar land slipping away.

Like unwanted efforts to pair you
with other old survivors,
first dressing you like a favored doll,
then inviting others to the tea party,
arriving in their own disguises.

And for what?
A moment, maybe, where we see each other unclothed
and barely recognizable as something once good?

These are the dried dates of inhospitable climes.
Bobbing for love in the Dead Sea,
lying down in parched pastures.

In the dark I'm squinting at a
full screen of widows in Windows,
people looking for partners
in a yearbook of aging ingénues,
with the faces of once promising students
now gone tharn,
permanently held back here
first for one year, then maybe two.

These are the back sides of half-lives,
begun, lived, and set aside.
On this night I will pick no partner,
but switch the screen to black.

I breathe in. I breathe out. I am OK in our sleepy house,
hushed now but sweetened still
by old shed skin and grains of memory dust,
fragrant, settled
permanently in.

Knowing What You're Made Of

There's a value, I suppose,
to knowing the core of things.

To my nephew I was making the case
why he must return to the VA hospital.
In exasperation I said the same as everyone:
that he came back a person different
than the one who went.

He looked amazed.
"Well sure. Now I'm made out of
mostly titanium and dead people."

And so for him
each day the IED blows,
though this time without surprise,
detonating remotely, I see,
in the depths behind his eyes.

Cut loose by the Percocet,
Demerol and Vicodin
he watches himself from outside his body
ambling a fairgrounds midway
lapsing into and lapsing out of
imagined carnival scenes:
a volunteer is called from the audience
and stands awkwardly on stage.
Unpracticed, picked at random,
but then whoosh...vanishes in a bang,
as if something he were born to do.

Leaving in the grass, dazzled gawkers
straining to understand what they just saw:
that super men, in hero armor,
can float up so high, be carried off so far on cue
with just the wave of a hand.

Fish, Cows, Pigs, and Chickens

Even without knowing ages, names or genders
I ate them all, two by two in a textbook march of species
from ark to fork at the Golden Corral.

It is a smorgasbord of mixed metaphors
touting 100 desserts, endless salad bar,
then blooded animals
collected from around the world:
gutted, skinned and plucked
sliced, boned, filleted, ground and quartered
baked and boiled, fried, steamed and chewed.

A heavenly host for beasts and those who love them.
Bathed in golden light, the Corral
proffers neither conversation nor family fun;
only a global range of carnage,
wide enough to slake
even rangy western appetites.

I finally stand, loosen my pants, buckle up and drive
with a menagerie riding high above my thighs,
beginning to quarrel beneath restraints.
Tomorrow (though not in a happy ceremony)
I will release them back into the wild
returning to the Earth what is the Earth's
to the sky what is the sky's
and whatever swims to the water's edge
before the cycle starts anew.

The Rocket Club
For the Isolatos MC

Today we pay a higher price
to remain Demons of Danger.

Old men with motorcycles -- expensive, fast --
that admittedly deserve to be exercised
by younger guys
who better complement the styling,
like slivers of tank chrome on lacquer at night.

Sometimes I fear we have become circus bears,
disproportioned with saggy asses
balanced on a preposterously small seat,
in a ring circling
at the frayed rope's end.

But I know we are something finer.
Like Pecos Bill who lassoed a twister,
we are astride
what remains of wild dreams.
Buying and seizing the last best chance
for speed and grace.
It is a trade we can afford to make.

When younger I used to fear
broken bones stemming from a crash.
Today I would just become a puff of powder
like a gag golf ball hit.
Or with one good blow take to the air
like white-headed dandelion fluff
riding invisible thermal rills
and landing like Dorothy did one day,
somewhere else
and very, very far away.

She Could Light Up a Room

You should know this.
The woman you adore
can light up a room,
just by walking across the floor
and throwing a switch.

Or she could light up a room
with a single match.

But more than that,
she could light up a whole house
with a can of gas and a few cloth scraps.

Or burn up and burn down
everything in your hometown.
She dreams, you see, of ended lives
and ashen faces behind her eyes.

Tonight, for you, bright she blazes.
But her days, my friend,
are spent in darker places.

Husbands Lost in Florida

They are still great destroyers of good women,
no longer deflowering, but widowing their wives.
Men shuffle and mill at heaven's gate,
like a mass beaching before the Pro Shop door.

On the days men die they reveal their true selves,
sneaking off with tasks half-done,
never fulfilling all she wished
or even what he promised.
But the hatchet is buried now from that old war.

Soon she'll be moving, too, to a one-floor house
that will become her second story,
where the end will play out,
leaving behind friends and a few shaky men
who when husbands go away, seem to wander in.

But, she'll admit, in bed on some nights
on her lips she still feels a kiss, slight and thin
as if they are kids again practicing to get it right.
And a nagging reminder too, whenever she leaves,
to turn out the lights, because
money doesn't grow on trees.

As if he still is weighing in
while cruising by, enjoying his new infinity.
Where, after not hearing from him since forever,
he now wants to invite her out again. Aw Men.

To a Small White Dog Napping

This little white dog sleeping
suddenly bows its back
and flicks its forelegs out,
as straight and stiff
as if they are fins
on a whale breaching.

Though perhaps a sea dog in his dream,
drier days will overtake.
Little dog, we are entwined,
though your life is timed to end before mine
by way of cars
or by disease of many kinds.

I have visited that sad space before
where the heart breaks in waves,
collapsing chamber-on-chamber in its core.

But standing between our then is now,
a realm where you happily drift.
Where dreams make us more,
transforming you into
a dog of momentary astronomic proportions;
and transforming me
into a man who can
put away approaching loss,
and drowsy-stroke your warm coat soft,
suspended for awhile like you, mid-breach,
balanced between beginnings and ends.

All in Boxes

We've created a shantytown,
in our soon-to-be-homeless place
built of boxes inside our house
from tall and thin to short and squat,
a rust-colored, U-Haul brown cityscape.

It is, in a way, what we have been
moving toward for years.
Now finally packing up,
no longer backing out.

"How many times can we
try to start again?"
That's what you asked.
But there's time still left to begin.

I take your larger point.
Of course we are no longer young,
yet beautiful still in different ways
than we began.
To you, boxes are unfriendly shades
of winter grey,
without child faces popping out.

But we have not stopped living.
So, let's fill these
boxes olive drab,
then, as Coronado told,
move them to a city made of gold.

Mexico is just days away
where we can
unpack our lives, and learn
to live again, all in.

Visible Parts of the Invisible World

Every now and then something pops through,
the occasional UFO
from inside a thundercloud.
Or little things from the lens
of an atomic microscope,
suddenly focusing our eyes
on atoms and eves
that appeared nowhere until seconds ago.

Or visions from Hubble
where dreams once derided
go to glow
after busting from
the earth below.

So amidst all this
how did we not spy
what our colleagues readily saw through
naked eyes:

two highly visible co-workers
(you and me)
nebulous partners admired from afar,
fall in love while at work
plotting end-of-life trajectories
of decaying stars?

Life Among City Deer

They are resilient spirits, these city deer,
forever trapped here between
native people who moved out,
and HOAs that moved in.

Once stealthy shadows on forest floors,
city deer now stop to visit,
pausing between bird bath and baby pool,
to see the children off to school.

Yet between the horns and hooves
there is the ancient magic still
of hold-over beings
that stop us in our tracks.

Sometimes from places deep within
I dream of swapping lives with them,
to snort out mirrored clouds of smoke,
or don buckskin, winter-thick
and blood-warm across my back.

I could live inside their habitat,
in the wild patch behind my lot,
untouched save for distant
motor whines and tower lines;
there learn to low in deep grass,
and to feed among the tender vines.

Ancestors once sketched running deer on stone cave
walls. Graceful lines of fluid forms in soot and coal,
some with the shadow of a single man.

That could be who I am.
But would they lend
their deer life to me,
for a day or not at all?

Maybe, far back, they already
tried and left our tract
before evolving into something more.
Done with us now, but living near
to not forget how far they've come
or the little things they once found dear,
that require daily monitoring
through impossibly black convex eyes
and depths unfathomable
of understanding.

Performing The Last Offices

By the time I finally got my hands on you it was too late.
You were already dead
with a rubber wedge beneath your head,
like no pillow you ever knew.
I am performing the last offices
before you move on,
after washing the world away.

I don't know for what name
the letter on your wristband stands,
nor where or why you lived or died.
But, unlike others I've prepared,
you lived fewer years
and retained more outward beauty signs.
I find those places and wash them one by one
as your mother, were she here,
surely would have done.

I dab the hollows of your hand
and smooth your fingers
long and thin,
to help your virtues show;
your best skin,
doing still what beauty can.

Many who I wash, I've readily forgot.
You, I may not.
I'm already wondering what if
your life and mine
had not unwound this far before we met,
before your organs were gathered
in a plastic sack and sewn back,
to travel with you like a hobo's pack.

And for awhile, too, perhaps I'll recall
a passing whim, wishing we could have been
both fully present here.

I hope you feel the tenderness
and through me know
that the rest of the world,
despite your early end,
held you too,
for every single second
it was allowed.

ACKNOWLEDGEMENTS

Poems in the *Dancing Naked in Front of Dogs* collection were written in Florida and Ohio over a period of six years, from 2013 through 2018. Assisting me during that time were:

My family, and especially my wife Sharon, a talented bookmaker who helped me organize the collected poems into a book, then assisted in its production;

The vastly gifted memoirist, poet and award-winning columnist Steve Kissing who has proffered both invaluable advice and lasting friendship;

My mother Ruth, the first poet I knew and the person who made me fall in love with words;

Members of the Ringling Museum Café Poets in Sarasota, who watched as many of these works grew through their awkward teenage years;

And many others who freely gave encouragement, kindness, honesty, support and opportunity precisely when needed.

Michael Maul

PUBLICATION CREDITS

Many of the poems included in this collection previously appeared in literary journals, reviews, and other publications in the USA and abroad. These include:

Avalon Literary Review: "Moving Parts"
The Adirondack Review: "The Clothes of Children Claimed by Fire"
Big River Poetry Review: "Fish, Cows, Pigs, and Chickens," "Dried Dates"
Bitterzoet Magazine: "Knowing What You're Made Of," "A Reporter's Poem," "Body Heat," "Old Shirt Paint"
Blue Lake Review: "No Cover Art"
BMW Owners News: "The Rocket Club"
Boston Literary Magazine: "Husbands Lost in Florida"
Clementine Unbound: "Anniversary Poem"
Dodging The Rain: "The Frère Jacques Men's Chorus"
Firewords: "Things I Know for Semi-Sure"
Front Porch Review: "Life Among City Deer," "Return to Hunan University"
Gravel Literary Magazine: "Blueberry Sorting"
Gyroscope Review: "Plane Crash, Malaysia Airlines," "Remnants"
Linden Avenue Literary Journal: "Chasing the Ex"
Montucky Review: "Sunday Clothes"
Pentimento Magazine: "Wedding Bouquet"
Remington Review: "What Haunts Us Most"
Stonecoast Review: "Spring Cuttings"
Uppagus: "Hand Knitting"
Vine Leaves Literary Journal: "To My Students"
Young Ravens Literary Review: "Germantown"

PHOTO CREDITS

Page 2: Provided by author
Page 22: Christian Vieler Photography
Page 44: Provided by author
Page 68: istockphoto.com

 Michael Maul resides in Bradenton, Florida, living near Sarasota Bay. His poems have previously appeared in numerous literary publications and anthologies in the U.S. as well as in Ireland, Scotland, and Australia.

He is also a past winner of the Mercantile Library Prize for Fiction, for a short story set in Siesta Key, and his work was selected for inclusion in *Intro 4*, an anthology of new voices published by The University of Virginia Press.

Maul is a graduate of the Ohio University creative writing program, where he earned bachelor's and master's degrees. He later held faculty and administrative positions at Ohio University (Athens, Ohio,) The Columbus College of Art and Design (Columbus, Ohio,) and Saint Louis University (St. Louis, Missouri.)